You Are Too a
Bully!

MaryAnn Milton Butterfield

abbott press®
A DIVISION OF WRITER'S DIGEST

Abbott Press books may be ordered through booksellers or by contacting:

Abbott Press
1663 Liberty Drive
Bloomington, IN 47403
www.abbottpress.com
Phone: 1-866-697-5310

Because of the dynamic nature of the Internet, any web addresses or links contained in this book may have changed since publication and may no longer be valid. The views expressed in this work are solely those of the author and do not necessarily reflect the views of the publisher, and the publisher hereby disclaims any responsibility for them.

Any people depicted in stock imagery provided by Thinkstock are models, and such images are being used for illustrative purposes only.

Certain stock imagery © Thinkstock.

ISBN: 978-1-4582-0969-6 (sc)
ISBN: 978-1-4582-0968-9 (hc)
ISBN: 978-1-4582-0967-2 (e)

Library of Congress Control Number: 2013910081

Printed in the United States of America.

Abbott Press rev. date: 6/26/2013

Table of Contents

Illustrations

Dedicated to

all who have been bullied—and to those who can help prevent future bullying

Acknowledgments

I am eternally grateful to my husband, Bob, for his steadfast support and encouragement as I wrote and rewrote, and he read and reread, story after story. I also wish to acknowledge my family: son Stuart and daughter-in-law Leslie and their sons, Andrew and Matthew; son Bob and his children, Meleanna and Robby, who not only supported and encouraged me but gave me raw material for a library of stories!

Thank you to my friends in Southwest Manuscripters in Torrance/Palos Verdes, California, where I first ventured into fiction writing. Spending hours in critique groups and learning to accept criticism helped me to appreciate the genre, as did hearing stimulating guest speakers, including member Ray Bradbury who chided, "For God's sake, finish things"—something I took to heart.

Most especially, I thank the generous members of the South Bay Critique Group of Manhattan Beach—Barbra Simpson, hostess, writer, artist, musician extraordinaire; Jalé Pullen (author of *The Sultan's Fingers*); and Devi Anton Anderson (author of *Shadow Trap*). We were a unique blend of writers with one mission: to help each other put forth the best stories we had in us.

I also appreciate the guidance and support I received from the Society of Children's Book Writers and Illustrators. As a member for years, I attended many summer conferences in Los Angeles, California. The how-to seminars conducted by professionals and writers who were successful in becoming published were invaluable.

Characters

Michael Kim, the protagonist

Jason Lewis, Michael's best friend

Chuck Howard, the bully (antagonist)

Mrs. Murphy, the school bus driver

Mrs. Ballou, Michael's teacher

Mr. Watt, the principal of Federal Street Elementary School

Eddie, the seat saver

Joel, a buddy

Robby, a buddy

Nicole, the hall monitor

Mr. Lewis (Stuart), Jason's dad

Mr. Kim (Matt), Michael's dad

Mrs. Kim, Michael's mom

Andy, Michael's escort to the school nurse

Ms. Jeanne, the school nurse

Mrs. Leslie, owner of the ruined garden

Mr. and Mrs. Howard, Chuck's parents

Chapter 1

Don't Call Me Chung King

Michael Kim pulled a pillow over his head, trying to drown out the buzzing of the alarm clock. He hated the sound, but now that he was twelve years old, Dad said it was time to "experience" getting up by himself. After all, hadn't Dad begun using an alarm clock when he was only eight? *Yeah, right! Like I believe that!* Grumbling, Michael swung his legs over the side of the bed, sat up, and smacked the button. He rubbed the sleep from his eyes.

I wish it was still vacation time. I hate being a new kid at this school. Of all the schools in the world, I get to go to one where there aren't many other Asians. At least Jason and his family are cool. Jason! I've gotta hurry. He said he'd wait with me at the bus stop so those big kids wouldn't pick on me like yesterday

———◄○►———

Michael finished his orange juice in five gulps and knocked over the glass as he put it down. "Oops. Sorry!"

"Michael!"

"It's okay, Mom; it's empty."

"Please, slow down! The bus doesn't come for another fifteen minutes."

"I know, but I told Jason I'd meet him early. It's really important."

"Okay, but *promise* to watch what you're doing, honey."

"I promise, Mom!" Michael picked up his backpack and raced out the back door. "Bye."

The same kids from yesterday were hanging around the bus stop. *Lucky me! I get to ride the bus with them every day for the rest of my life!* Michael slowed his walk. *Gosh, where is Jason?*

"Hey, it's Chung King," a tall boy with blond hair called out, pointing and laughing at Michael. The kids with him looked and laughed but didn't say anything.

"I told you, that's not my name!" Michael snarled. Jason ran up, gasping to catch his breath. "Aw, don't pay any attention to Chuck. He thinks he's funny, but everyone else knows he's a jerk."

"How come you're so late?"

"I had to run back for my lunch." Jason hopped around pretending to box Michael. "Hey, aren't you excited about this weekend?" His face was flushed from running, and his eyes danced. "I can't wait to work on the fort. It's all I've been thinking about."

Michael bobbed his head and pretended to box back. "Me too! I hope our parents will let us sleep in it when it's finished. That'd be so cool!"

The big yellow school bus clattered up the street and pulled to a stop. Flashing lights and squealing brakes caught the boys' attention as the doors hissed open and folded back.

Michael clambered up the steps with Jason right behind him. "Morning, Mrs. Murphy."

"Well, the top o' the mornin' to you both!" Mrs. Murphy's Irish brogue filled the bus.

Michael and Jason took the first empty seats.

"We need to make our fort big enough to fit us and some of our friends—like maybe Joel and Eddie," Michael declared.

"Yeah, but don't forget Robby. He's cool." Jason grinned. "But no girls allowed unless we *both* say it's okay. Right?"

"Right!"

3

Reaching school, Michael made Jason wait until Chuck and the older boys were off the bus.

"I'm glad we both go to the same school, even if we aren't in the same class," Jason said as they headed up the walkway and into school.

"Yeah, me too!"

Mrs. Ballou stood at the doorway to the classroom. "Good morning, Michael." She rested a hand on his shoulder and called out, "Everyone please take a seat and settle down quickly."

Michael looked up. "Is today when you said we're gonna have activity time?"

"Yes, it is, but only if we get all our work done."

"Yippee!" Michael's eyes glowed. "I know *exactly* what I'm gonna make—a diorama of the fort Jason and I are gonna build with our dads this weekend!"

Mrs. Ballou smiled. "Do we have the materials you'll need to make a fort?"

"All I need are Popsicle sticks. Oh, and some glue and a piece of cardboard. The cardboard's gonna be the ground, the Popsicle sticks will be the boards, and the glue will be the nails, and maybe I can paint it too."

"That's a fine idea."

At the end of the day, Michael crammed his books and homework into his backpack. *I can zip up the diorama in my jacket to carry it on the bus. That way, it won't get broken.* He grinned. *Joel and Robby liked it, but just wait until Jason sees it! He's gonna freak.*

When Mrs. Ballou excused the class, Joel and Robby followed Michael into the hallway to look for Jason.

"Yo, Chung King!" called a voice from down the hallway.

It was Chuck.

"Don't call me that! I keep telling you. My name is Michael."

The boy laughed and pointed at Michael's jacket. "Hey, whatcha got in there, Chung King?"

"Nothing!"

"Nothing? Come on, Chung King! Show me whatcha got in there." He danced around Michael while patting him on the head. "Nothing? You sure?"

"Get away from him," Robby insisted.

The boy clapped his hands loudly right under Michael's nose and hip-bumped against him.

"Stop it. It's a diorama, and you're gonna break it."

"What's going on, you guys?" the hall monitor demanded.

"Chuck's picking on Michael, Nicole," Joel said.

Chuck glared at Joel. "Am not! I'm just teasing." He stared at Michael, unsmiling. "Just having some fun with my little buddy here, right?"

Michael swallowed. *I should tell her.*

Michael hiding the fort diorama from Chuck

When Michael didn't answer, the girl said, "Chuck, you know better than to fool around in the hallway."

She looked at Michael. "You're new, but you need to follow the rules too, or I'll have to put you on report."

"But Nicole, it wasn't him—" insisted Joel.

"Well, you were all involved, and if it happens again, I'll put you *all* on report." She lifted her nose in the air and adjusted the hall monitor sash across her chest. "It's my job to see that you follow the rules."

Another boy grabbed Chuck's arm. "Hey, come on. The bus is almost here." Turning to Michael, he said, "Hey, kid, don't mind Chuck; he's only kidding around."

Michael turned his back. *Yeah, right! I'd like to tell stupid Chuck he's not funny. He's just a jerk!*

Chuck grinned. "Yeah, Chung King, can't ya take a little joke?"

Michael glared in return.

"Come on." Joel tugged Michael's sleeve. "There's Jason. Let's go show him your fort."

"Yeah! Hey Jason," Robby hollered. "Over here."

Jason looked at the big boys and then back at Michael.

"What's the matter?"

"Chuck's been picking on Michael again," offered Joel.

7

"Oh, don't pay any attention to him." Jason put his arm around Michael's shoulders. "Everyone knows Chuck's a jerk!"

Michael nodded his head, agreeing, and then remembered the surprise he was holding. "Hey, Jason, wait 'til you see what I've got."

"What?"

"I'll show you on the bus."

"But what is it?"

"A diorama of our fort!"

"Awww, ya told him," Joel cried. "Ya shoulda made him guess."

"You're kidding. A diorama? Really, Michael?"

"He made it during activity time," Robby said. "It is so cool."

As usual, Chuck and his friends crowded to the front of the line to grab the backseats on the bus. Michael and Jason took their time boarding so they could sit closer to the front.

Once seated, Michael carefully unzipped the jacket. "The glue might not be hard yet, so don't touch it, okay?"

"I won't! Just show me."

Michael lifted the diorama from his jacket.

"Wow!" Jason's eyes went round with excitement. "That's so cool! And it's just how we planned it." He turned partway around in the seat. "You guys want to see what our fort is gonna look like?"

Robby and Joel peeked over the seat. "Wow! Has Eddie seen it?"

"Not yet. Get his attention and tell him to look." Jason turned back around. "Hold it up high so Eddie can see, Michael."

Eddie stood to see over the seat. "That's so cool!"

Michael laughed, enjoying the attention, and rewrapped the diorama to protect it. When the bus stopped, he and Jason stayed seated until the older boys had left by the rear doors.

"I'm gonna hurry home before something happens to this. See ya tomorrow, Jason."

Racing up the street, Michael entered the house through the back door and dropped his backpack on the floor. "I'm home!"

He opened the jacket on the kitchen table, removing the diorama carefully. *Good. It's still in one piece.* He traced the outline of the roof with his fingers and grinned. *Wait 'til Dad sees this!*

"Hi, honey!" Michael's mom grabbed him from behind in a bear hug. "How was school?"

"It was good—" Michael frowned. "I guess."

"Just good?" she pressed. "I thought you loved your teacher and all the new friends you made this summer."

"I do."

"Then what's the matter?"

"I don't know." Michael picked at a hangnail.

"Hey, talk to me for a minute. Is it something I can help you with?"

"Not really. It's just there's this kid named Chuck that I don't like."

"Why is that?"

"Aw, he keeps bugging me."

Frowning, his mother asked, "How so, Michael?"

"He keeps calling me 'Chung King,' and I don't like it."

Mom chuckled.

"Mo-om! It's not funny! I *really* don't like it. What does it mean, anyway?"

"You're right. I guess it isn't funny to you. I was laughing because he's teasing you with a Chinese name. Chung King is an old brand name of canned Chinese food."

"Oh brother! I'm Korean, not Chinese!"

"I know, sweetheart, but the boy may not know the difference between Korean and Chinese or Japanese or Vietnamese. There aren't many Asians in this community, and it could be that you're the first Korean boy he's ever met."

"I don't care; I still don't like it. He wouldn't like it if I did it to him!"

Mom opened a bag of cookies and offered one to Michael.

"I understand. How about telling the boy nicely that you don't like it?"

"That doesn't work, 'cause I already did ten times."

"Perhaps you should ignore the boy. If he thinks the name doesn't bother you anymore, he'll probably stop."

"Not this guy!" Michael sighed. *I can't talk to her 'cause she doesn't know what a jerk Chuck is. She always says, "Sticks and stones will break your bones, but names will never hurt you." But that's not true. Names hurt me, and I hate it.*

"Now tell me about what you have here." She gave Michael's shoulder a gentle squeeze. "Did you make it?"

"Yes, it's the diorama for the fort me and Jason and Dad are going to build this weekend."

"Jason and I ..." his mother corrected.

"Yeah, Jason and I." *And we're never gonna let Chuck in it either!*

Chapter 2

Scared

The next morning, Michael wasn't in any hurry to see Chuck or the other big kids at the bus stop. He hung out in the garage until Jason showed up and then dashed out.

As always, the big kids pushed to get on the bus first and took seats in the rear. Mrs. Murphy's deep laugh filled the bus. "Good mornin', lads."

"Let's sit up front, Jason," Michael said, tugging on Jason's sleeve. "And let's always be the last ones off, okay?" Michael felt better sitting near Mrs. Murphy. She was a lot of fun, but she made everyone obey the rules too.

"Sure."

When the bus was empty, Jason yelled, "Come on!" He rushed into the aisle and down the first three steps ahead of Michael and stopped. They jumped the last step together. Mrs. Murphy cranked the door closed and pulled away.

A familiar voice startled Michael. "Hey, Chung King, ya trying to hide from me?"

"Go away, and stop calling me that!" Michael hollered.

Chuck was holding his sides, doubled over laughing. "Man, you jumped three feet in the air. Three feet! You shoulda seen yourself."

"Leave him alone," Jason yelled. "You're not funny."

"Ha ha ha."

"Michael, why does he always say Chung King? What's that mean, anyway?" asked Jason.

"He thinks I'm Chinese, but I'm not. I'm Korean!" Michael scowled at Chuck and pulled Jason's arm to hurry him along.

"Aw, he's just a jerk. Anyway, what's the difference between being Korean or Chinese?" asked Jason.

"It's kind of like how the United States and Canada are both American countries, but they're different. Korea is an Asian country, like China and Japan and stuff. There's a difference in all of them." Michael shrugged. "I don't know how to explain it exactly, except my grandparents were born across the ocean in Korea and then came over here to live."

"Mine did too, but from Europe," Jason said. "My dad says I'm half English and half Irish."

"That's why your skin is white and mine isn't," Michael said, holding his bare arm up to Jason's.

"Not in the summer; look!" Jason put his tanned arm against Michael's. "We're the same color in the summer!"

"We're twins." Michael laughed. "But then you'd have to have different-shaped eyes too."

"I wonder why that is?" Jason studied Michael's eyes. "But who cares?"

"I dunno."

Michael and Jason made it to their classrooms just in time for the bell. Mrs. Ballou flashed a big smile at Michael as he pulled the door closed behind him.

Later in the day, Michael got to thinking about Chuck. *He sure scared me this morning when he jumped out from behind the bus. I hope he doesn't do anything this afternoon. I wish we weren't the first and last stops and he didn't ride on my bus. It would be more fun if Robby and Joel were at our stop instead of him.*

Just before dismissal, Mrs. Ballou called Michael up to her desk. "Is anything wrong? You were in such a happy mood this morning, but now something seems to be bothering you. Is there anything you want to talk about?

Michael hesitated. *She'll probably just think I'm dumb 'cause I don't like being called names.* "I'm okay, Mrs. Ballou. Thanks." He loaded his backpack slowly, stalling for time.

Jason came to the doorway. "Hurry up, Michael, or we'll miss the bus."

"I don't want to hurry," Michael whispered. "If Chuck sees me, he'll probably do something again."

"No he won't, 'cause I'll be with you." Jason shrugged. "Besides, you can tell Mrs. Murphy if he bugs you on the bus."

"*No!* And don't you tell either!"

"Gosh, Michael, okay. You don't have to get so mad."

"I'm sorry, Jason. Let's just forget about it, okay?"

On the bus, Michael and Jason took the seats behind Mrs. Murphy, who was watching them in a wide rearview mirror.

"Why so glum, chums?"

Michael sank low in his seat. "I'm okay." He felt everyone was looking at them. Luckily, the bus monitor interrupted Mrs. Murphy and waved her to move on.

"Hey, Michael," Eddie called out. "When're you gonna start building the fort?"

"My dad said we can do it this weekend because it's a holiday weekend."

"My dad's gonna help," added Jason.

"Wish we could help." The bus pulled up to a stop. "See you, guys!" Robby and Eddie said as they scrambled out the back door of the bus.

Michael nudged Jason. "Let's get off fast this time and run up our street before Chuck gets off."

"Sure!"

The bus drew up to the curb, and the boys rushed forward. Michael glanced back at Chuck.

"Slow down, boys," bellowed Mrs. Murphy. "You aren't going to a fire."

Jason stopped short at her command, and Michael plowed right into him. They both fell down in the aisle.

"Mother of Mercy, that's exactly why I want you to take your time," Mrs. Murphy said, shaking her head. "You boys okay?"

"Yes, Mrs. Murphy. Sorry."

Jason poked his head out of the front bus exit. "Hey, he's not here, Michael. He's gone. Come on."

"Who's not there? Is something wrong, Michael?" demanded Mrs. Murphy.

"Nope." Michael grinned at her and stepped out of the bus. "Bye, Mrs. Murphy. Thanks."

Jason walked up the street with Michael, relieved that Chuck was not in sight.

"My dad said we could probably build the fort in two weekends," Jason said, kicking a stone in the air.

"Yeah, my dad did too. He already cut the windows and door out of big pieces of plywood. Now all we gotta do is put the pieces together. Just like my diorama."

"I wish we could start it right now!"

Michael laughed. "I know. Me too!"

"Agggh! Caught you, Chung King!" Chuck bellowed, jumping from behind a shaggy hedge.

The boys shrieked. Michael dropped his backpack in the street as they ran away, but he was too scared to go back for it. Looking back, he saw Chuck standing there laughing, so he kept running.

"H-e-e-e's such a jerk," stammered Jason.

"I *told* you!" Michael panted, holding his side. It hurt from running so fast.

"What about your backpack?"

"I'll get it after he's gone."

"But what if he takes it?"

"He better not!" Michael looked back down the street.

"You should tell someone."

"No! And don't you either."

"Okay, it's your backpack and your butt when your parents find out you lost it."

Michael continued around to the back of his house and opened the kitchen door. He went straight to the refrigerator and opened it. "Hi, I'm home."

His mom sneaked up from behind and planted a big kiss on his cheek. "Hi, sweetheart."

"Mom! I'm a guy," he said, trying to rub the kiss off with the back of his hand.

"Yes, and you're *my* guy!" she said, squeezing him in a hug. "How come you're so sweaty?"

"Jason and I raced each other home."

"Where's your backpack?"

"Ummm, I guess I forgot it."

"On the bus?"

"Ummm, down the street."

"Then you go right back and get it."

"Okay. Wanna go with me?"

"I have cookies in the oven. You run along and get it before it disappears."

Michael went to the garage door and peeked out. He felt sick to his stomach. The coast looked clear, so he ran down to the spot where he'd dropped the backpack. It wasn't there! Looking around, he found it leaning against a lamppost on the sidewalk, but his papers were scattered all over the street. Tears stung his eyes and made his nose run. *I hate Chuck!* He wiped his nose on his sleeve as he gathered up the papers and raced home.

Chapter 3

Building the Fort

Michael called Jason early Saturday morning. "We're ready to start on the fort; are you?"

"Yup, my dad's getting the nail gun, and we'll be right over."

"Dad, Jason, and Mr. Lewis are on their way," Michael yelled.

"Okay, so let's head out and start clearing the site." Michael shot out the kitchen door.

Dad looked at Mom and laughed. "I think this is the most excited I've seen him since he got his racing bike."

At the same time, Jason tore through the gate at the side of the house ahead of his dad. "Where do we start?"

Mr. Kim laughed. "Hi, Stu, Jason. Well, I thought you could work with me to cut down these scrub trees, and Michael can help Mr. Lewis pull up the weeds and brush. Is that okay with you, Stu?"

"Sounds great." Mr. Lewis handed Michael and Jason some extra gloves from his toolbox. "Put these on so you won't get splinters."

"Gee, thanks." Michael's pair fit him perfectly.

"Can I use this, Mr. Kim?" Jason held up a small handsaw.

"Yes. Do you know how?"

"Um, kinda."

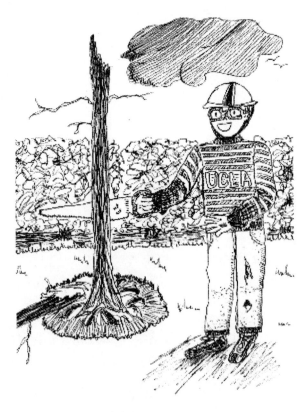

Learning to use a saw

"Here, let me hold the middle of the tree, and you can begin sawing near the bottom. Just drag the blade back across the bark to get a groove started. Now push it forward. Keep it up, and try to get a rhythm going as you saw back and forth. Let the saw do the work."

After a few shaky strokes, Jason got a good rhythm going.

"That's right!" Mr. Kim beamed. "You've got it!"

Once the brush and trees were cleared, Mr. Lewis and Michael dug up rocks and carried them to a back corner of the yard. They used shovels to pat the dirt smooth, and the boys jumped up and down to tamp it flat.

"I think that's about it, Matt, don't you?" Mr. Lewis asked Mr. Kim, wiping the sweat from his forehead with a handkerchief.

"Yeah, the ground looks great, Stu. Let's measure the area where the floor will go and put double stakes at each corner."

Mr. Lewis handed a spool to Michael. "Michael and Jason, tie this twine to that stake and then run it from stake to stake to form a rectangle."

"What's that for, Dad?" Jason scrunched his nose.

"It outlines the spot for the fort," Michael said. "Right, Mr. Lewis?"

"Right you are, Michael, and when you boys are done, we'll be ready to start putting things together."

Mr. Kim nodded to Mr. Lewis. "Can you help me carry the large sections of plywood out from the basement?"

"Sure."

"The wood is cut to size," Mr. Kim said, "and I've numbered the pieces." He rubbed his back. "If we lay out the pieces in numerical order, it should go together pretty smoothly."

"I'll say," Mr. Lewis said. "Even the window holes are cut out. Good thinking, Matt!"

"Thanks. Whew. Let's take a break after this."

They all washed their hands with water from the garden hose and devoured the chicken salad sandwiches Mrs. Kim served to them on the patio.

"Okay, what's next?" Jason asked, swallowing the last bite of pickle and grinning at Mr. Kim.

Mr. Kim glanced at Mr. Lewis. "Does he do his homework with this much enthusiasm?"

"No way!" Mr. Lewis shook his head and laughed.

"All right, here's the plan." Mr. Kim rolled out a large piece of paper on the picnic table. "See these little rectangles? They represent bricks. Think you boys can follow this plan and place the bricks inside the lines of twine just like this diagram shows?"

"Sure!" The boys ran to the pile of bricks and began placing them in an *X* pattern.

"That looks good. Now, put a row around the outer edge. The bricks will support the floorboard and allow air to circulate so the wood won't get wet and rot." Mr. Lewis handed the boys the rest of the bricks.

"Okay, boys, step back for a minute. Stu, can you grab the other end of this piece?"

Together the men laid the large piece of plywood marked #1 on top of the bricks.

"We now have a floor," said Mr. Kim.

The piece fit perfectly inside the twine lines, flush up against the stakes.

Mr. Lewis used his nail gun to anchor the floor to the corner stakes. "This is temporary and will hold the floorboard in place while we build up the sides. Once the fort is up, we'll remove the stakes."

Pieces two and three were nailed to the floorboard. By late afternoon, the four sides were in place and the shell of the fort was formed.

Laying the bricks using the diagram

"Great job, everyone," Mr. Kim said, "but it's time to quit for today."

"When are we going to work on it again, Dad?" pressed Michael. "Tomorrow?"

"We'll have to see. But it will be *after* church and homework."

Mr. Lewis pulled the bill of Jason's hat down over his eyes. "Same goes for you, kiddo."

The boys made faces at each other.

"Excuse me, Mr. Kim," Jason said, "but can we take one last ride to the park before we have to go in for dinner?"

"It's okay with me." Mr. Kim raised his eyebrows and looked at Mr. Lewis.

"Yes. It's okay with me too, but watch the time." Mr. Lewis shook his head. "Where do they get that energy?"

The boys dashed around the house to the garage. Michael straddled his bike. "Hop on the back, Jason, and I'll give you a ride to your house."

Jason's bike was lying on the grass in his front yard. He stood it up and swung his leg over the seat.

"Race ya," Michael called out, standing on his pedals to go faster.

"No fair! You got a head start!" Jason pedaled hard. "Hey, wait up! I've got an idea."

Michael slowed down. "What kind of idea?"

"Maybe we could start a club."

"Yeah, maybe. But only with people we both like." Michael zigzagged his bicycle slowly, thinking about who he'd want to let join.

Jason bent low over the handlebars and pumped as fast as he could to get ahead of Michael. "Race ya!" he shouted as he zoomed out in front.

"Hey, no fair!" Michael hooted and chased after him.

They sped around the corner and up the drive into the park.

Across the street, riding toward them, was Chuck.

They both saw him at the same time. Michael's heart skipped a beat. "Jason, let's get outta here."

"Okay. I'm right behind you."

The boys turned away sharply. Their screeching tires left black skid marks on the pavement as they raced away as fast as they could. When they looked back to see if Chuck was following them, they were surprised to find he wasn't. Instead, Chuck sat straddling his bike, his head thrown back, and he was laughing and hollering at them.

"Chung King and Dog Food, come on back! *Ha ha ha ha ha*!" He laughed.

"Did he just call you Dog Food?" Michael panted.

"Yeah, and he called you Chung King."

"He's nuts."

"Yeah."

The boys fishtailed onto the driveway at Michael's house just as Mr. Lewis rounded the corner from the backyard.

"Whoa! Where's the fire?" Mr. Lewis pointed at the marks on the driveway. "Those tires aren't going to last if you keep riding like that."

"Sorry, Mr. Lewis." Michael looked at Jason to see if he was going to say anything.

"Yeah, I guess we were going a lot faster than we thought." Jason held up his hand for a high five. "See ya, Michael."

Michael returned the high five. "Yeah, see ya, Jason. Bye, Mr. Lewis."

The next afternoon Michael helped his dad work on the fort.

"It isn't finished, Michael, so I don't want anybody climbing up on it yet." Dad took off his work gloves and looked at the work they'd done. Pleased, he said, "We'll finish it up another day, but right now, Mom and I have some other things we need to do."

"Awww, do ya hafta?"

"Hey, we have a long weekend coming up. We'll finish it then, sport." His dad laughed. "And don't you have some homework to finish?"

"I already did it." Michael shoved his hands in his pockets and poked at a hole in the ground with the toe of his sneaker. "Jason and I just really wanted to play in it today."

"You *can* play inside it; you just can't get up on *top* yet."

"Really? Can I go call Jason?"

"Sure. And if Mr. Lewis has some time next weekend, we can stabilize the railings and finish things up then."

"Yesss!" Michael raced into the house.

———◀◦▶———

Michael and Jason carried boxes of army men, tanks, airplanes, and trucks into the fort. They set them all up like a military base, with a medic station, landing strip, and a place for helicopters to land. Their military men and fortified base would protect all the houses on Wilson Avenue from an invading army or air raid.

Jason sat back on his heels. "What are we gonna do about Chuck?"

Michael scowled. "Whaddaya mean?"

"Well, we can't let him keep chasing us off our own street or let him keep calling us dumb names."

"Names don't hurt."

"Well, maybe not you, but nobody called you Dog Food!"

"That *was* kind of funny. *Woof woof.* Where does he get these names, anyway?" Michael giggled.

"Well, I don't like it, and don't 'woof woof' me!" Jason made a fist and pretended to throw a punch. "We've gotta do something!"

"Hey, you promised me—" began Michael.

"I know. But then *you've* gotta do something!"

"That's easy for you to say. But what can I do?" Michael tossed a miniature soldier from one hand to the other. The name-calling didn't seem so bad now that Chuck was calling Jason names too. *Golly, I hate Chuck for scaring me. Now Jason's bugging me. I wish everyone would just leave me alone.*

Chapter 4

Afraid to Go to School

Michael's mother touched his shoulder. "Time to get up, young man."

"I've got a stomachache," grumbled Michael. "I can't go to school. I think I'm sick."

"When did this start?" Mom felt his forehead. "You don't feel extra warm. Maybe your tummy is just hungry for the blueberry pancakes I made for breakfast."

"You made pancakes?"

"I sure did. You worked hard yesterday, so I thought you might like a hearty breakfast."

"Okay, maybe I'll try to go." *There's no way I'm missing Mom's pancakes.*

Michael bounded out of bed and rummaged in his dresser. He pulled on the first clothes he touched. In no time he was at the table digging into a stack of hot pancakes dripping with butter and maple syrup.

"Great breakfast, Mom!" Michael swallowed the last bite and gulped his milk. "See ya!"

"Thanks, honey. Have a great day."

"You too. Bye!"

Michael poked his head out of the garage several times and ran out when he saw Jason.

"Let's stay back a ways, Jason."

"Sure. Let the jerks get on first."

"Yeah, the stupid jerks!" Michael laughed and gave Jason a shove.

Jason shoved back. "Hold it. Here's the bus."

The boys thumped up the steps and took seats right behind the driver.

"Hey, Mrs. Murphy!"

"Good morning, boys." She raised one eyebrow and looked at Jason and then at Michael. "Anything going on with you two I should know about?"

"Yes. I mean, no. Everything's okay," Michael replied, picking at a fingernail. He nudged Jason in the ribs with his elbow.

"Yeah, we're okay, Mrs. Murphy." Jason scowled at Michael and gave him a hard nudge back.

"Okay, but you'd tell me if something wasn't." Mrs. Murphy paused, waiting for their answer. "Right?" she prodded.

"Yes," they answered together.

Jason whispered behind his hand, "You've gotta tell Mrs. Ballou."

"I can't. Besides, what if Chuck finds out I told? He'll just get mad and chase us or mess with my backpack again."

"But if Mrs. Ballou tells his teacher, then maybe they'll kick him off the bus!"

"Yeah, and then what?" Michael shrugged his shoulders. "He can still find me in the hallways or on our street."

The bus monitor was standing at the stop, so Chuck didn't have a chance to do anything. Yet all day Michael couldn't stop thinking about him.

What if everyone starts calling me Chung King? Golly, what if Jason tells on Chuck? He promised he wouldn't, but what if he gets scared? Gosh, my stomach really hurts. What's our homework? I forgot what she said. I have a headache.

"Michael, may I see you for a minute?" Mrs. Ballou's voice cut through the silence, and Michael jumped. "The rest of the class is free to leave *quietly* for recess."

Uh-oh, Jason musta told! Michael's face felt hot.

Mrs. Ballou waited until they were alone. "Are you feeling okay?"

"Um, yes."

"You don't seem yourself—is something bothering you?"

"No."

"Are you having a problem here at school?"

"Not really." Michael looked down at his dirty sneakers. His face was pink, but maybe she wouldn't notice.

"Okay." Mrs. Ballou paused and tapped her pencil on the desk. "But if you need some help, Michael, please let me know."

"Ummm—" He tried to tell her, but his mouth went dry. *I just can't. She'll think I'm such a baby.* "I will. Can I go out to recess now?" Michael was edging toward the door.

"Yes, of course."

After school, Michael waited in the classroom doorway and kept an eye out for Chuck. As soon as he saw Jason, he called him over. "Have you seen him yet?"

"No. Let's go hang around the bus monitor like we did yesterday."

"Okay." Michael wasn't sure this would work again.

"Don't look now, but Chuck's over on the grass, and it looks like he's looking for us," Jason whispered.

"Yeah, I saw him."

They stood still, keeping their eyes on Chuck so he couldn't sneak around behind them.

Chuck grinned, said something to his buddies, and pointed in Michael's direction. The other kids looked over and laughed.

"Don't look at him anymore, Michael. He's just a jerk."

"I know, but I can't help it. I have to see where he is so he can't scare me."

"Yeah, I guess."

On the way home, Michael and Jason sat quietly on the bus, staring out the window. Mrs. Murphy eyed them in the rearview mirror a couple of times but didn't say anything. The boys stalled as long as they could before getting off.

"So long boys," Mrs. Murphy called out before cranking the doors closed, leaving Michael and Jason on the street.

They checked all directions for Chuck. "Let's hurry," Michael said.

"Let's run, but on the other side of the street." Jason took off, and Michael had to sprint to keep up with him.

They paused for a second when they reached Michael's garage. "Chuck never comes up this far, so we're safe now."

"Just in case, I'm gonna keep running." Jason's words came out in gasps as he ran on.

"Me too. See ya." Michael darted behind his house and in the back door.

"I'm home," Michael called to his mother, heading to the cookie jar.

"Hi, honey. Wash those hands before you touch anything."

"Okay." Michael laughed. "You *always* say that."

Mrs. Kim poured two small glasses of milk and placed a napkin at two places. "I think I'll join you for a cookie."

Michael returned to the table with clean hands and grabbed a cookie, downing it in a couple of bites. "Yum, these are sooo good, Mom. I wish you'd make these every day!"

"Then you'd get tired of them."

"Uh-uh, not these." He licked the chocolate on his finger.

"Michael, is there anything you want to talk to me about?"

"No, except these cookies are *really* great."

Mom smiled. "Mrs. Ballou called today."

"She called you? Why? I told her everything's okay!"

"Well, she's concerned. You haven't seemed like yourself lately. You missed a couple of spelling words on a test and didn't finish some of your class work."

Michael struggled. *Should I tell Mom? No. I already did, and she wants me to just ignore Chuck so he'll stop. That might work for adults, but it didn't work with him.* "I don't know why it's such a big deal. It was only a practice test. Besides, I always get them right on the real test."

"It's not a big deal; it's just unusual."

Michael scowled. "Watch, I'll get all my work done tomorrow."

"Okay, honey, if you're sure."

The ring of the telephone interrupted them.

"I'll get it," Michael said, relieved to change the subject.

"Hello?"

"Hey, Chung King," a raspy voice whispered, "I've got your number now."

Michael hit the end-call button and slammed the telephone into its holder. "Wrong number, Mom."

Chapter 5

He Should Tell

Michael called Jason. "We've gotta make a plan. Chuck called me. He knows my number now and can bug me even more."

"Geez, that's creepy!" Jason snorted. "Hey, one thing we can do is get our friends to save us seats. This way, we can always sit behind Mrs. Murphy."

"Yeah, and every day we can do what we've been doin'—like wait with the bus monitor or wait to get off at the last minute." *But how's that gonna stop him from calling me?*

Their plan worked for a couple of days. Sometimes Chuck would walk close by the bus monitor and whisper, "Chung King." Afterward he'd hold his stomach and laugh his head off. Yet there were other times when he wouldn't pay any attention to them at all.

"It's Friday, Michael, and Chuck hasn't bothered us all week. Our plan's working."

"Yeah, I know. Let's forget about him. We've got three whole days now to work on our fort."

"A fort?" exclaimed one of the friends who saved their seats each day. "Did you say you guys are building a fort?"

"Well, our dads are really building it, but Jason and I are helping a lot. It's gonna be great, isn't it, Jason?"

"Yeah. The best! It has a floor and windows and everything."

"Can I come see it?"

"Me too?" asked another boy.

"After it's finished," Michael said.

"Yeah, we're going to start a club," added Jason.

Word spread quickly, and soon a number of kids wanted to know if they could join the new club.

"We'll let you know when it's finished. Our dads said they might get it done this weekend. Right, Jason?"

"Yeah, they said they'd try."

The boys jabbered excitedly as they exited the bus and scattered in different directions. "Don't forget to call me when it's ready," one boy yelled.

On the street, Chuck walked right up to Michael and Jason before they had a chance to start running.

"What's this about a fort, Chung King?" Chuck said, grinning. His thumbs were hooked on the belt loops of his jeans, and he rocked back on his heels, looking down at them.

Chuck being mean to Michael and Jason at the bus stop

"Nothing to you," Jason jeered.

Michael felt glued to the spot. His legs wouldn't move.

"Come on, Chung King. Ya holding out on me?" He tugged on Michael's arm.

"It's nothing." Michael pulled away and took off running toward home with Jason at his heels.

When they got to Michael's house, the boys looked back and saw Chuck was nowhere to be seen.

"Geezy, Jason, don't say stuff to make him mad."

"But the fort's not for him. You said so, Michael."

"I know. But now he knows about it. What if he does something to mess it up?"

"Like what?" Jason asked.

"How do I know? Like throwing dog poop inside or something?"

"Gross. You gotta tell your dad, Michael."

"He'll think I'm a tattling."

"No, he won't."

"He'll want to talk to Chuck, and that'll make it worse."

"Well, we aren't going to let Chuck in the fort, are we?" Jason asked.

"Nope, never!"

"If he does anything to it, then you *gotta* tell your dad who did it!" demanded Jason.

"I will."

"Okay, see ya."

"Tell your dad you want to come over early tomorrow," Michael called after him.

"I will."

Michael opened the back door and hollered, "I'm ho-ome." Dropping his backpack on the closest chair, he headed for the refrigerator.

"Hi, honey." Mrs. Kim enveloped him from behind in a big hug and nuzzled his neck.

"Awww, come on, Mom. I'm gonna spill." He giggled as he juggled the juice pitcher.

"How was school today?"

"Okay."

"What did you get on your spelling test?"

"One hundred percent!" He put his nose up in the air and gave her a smug smile.

"That's our boy. How about your math? Did you finish in class?"

"Yesss—and I did extra-credit problems."

"Okay! Good for you. Guess I should let you have that last cookie I'd saved for myself."

"There's only one left?" Michael's eyebrows shot up in surprise.

"They're your dad's favorites too, remember?"

"Shoot!"

The next morning Michael awakened to the scent of bacon wafting into his room. His tummy growled as he climbed out of bed and padded down the hallway to the kitchen.

"Good morning, young man," Dad said. "Mom's fixing us a special breakfast before we go out and tackle the fort!"

"I could tell. I smelled it in my room. Mornin', Mom."

"Good morning, honey. Before you sit down, how about pouring the orange juice for us?"

"Sure."

The telephone rang, and Michael just stared at it.

Mr. Kim looked over the top of his newspaper at Michael and nodded toward the phone. "Want to get that?"

"Umm, okay." Michael hoped Chuck wouldn't be up this early. "Hello?"

"Hey, Michael, my dad said to tell you we'll be over in thirty minutes."

"Great!" Michael gave a sigh of relief at the sound of Jason's voice.

After breakfast, the boys and their dads tackled the fort in earnest. They built a ladder with slats to go from the ground to the roof. Michael helped assemble sections of the railing, and Mr. Lewis drilled holes and screwed the laths in place. The dads hoisted the railing sections to the top of the fort and secured them to corner supports.

Mr. Kim let Jason use the power drill to prepare the holes for the screws on the door hinges, and Michael got to do the same for the window shutters.

Standing in the doorway of the fort, Mr. Kim drilled several holes on the outside on the door frame and affixed a bracket. He smiled at Michael's mom who had come into the yard to check on their project.

"What's that for, Dad?" asked Michael.

"Mom's made a surprise for you boys." He winked as Mrs. Kim, slipped something over a pole, and fit the pole into the bracket. A flag unfurled in the breeze, exposing an *M* and a *J* entwined. The navy-blue letters were centered on a bright red background.

"Hey, those are our initials," cried Jason.

"Cool," Michael said, admiring the flag. "Thanks, Mom, it looks great!"

"Yeah, Mrs. Kim, it's great. Thanks."

Mrs. Kim laughed. "I'm glad you like it, boys."

———◄o►———

That evening, Michael couldn't stop thinking about Chuck, and he couldn't get to sleep. *Sure was nice not having Chuck around. I wonder what he's gonna do to us next week? I wish he'd move to another school.* He tried to think of other things, but his mind kept going back to Chuck. He couldn't tell when he finally fell asleep, but when he woke up, he was still tired.

"Come on, Michael, or you'll be late for school." Mom shook his shoulder gently.

He wanted to say, "Good," but didn't.

"Awww, gee, Mom, can't I stay home one day?"

"Why?"

"Just to have a day off," he moaned. "I'm so tired."

His mom laughed. "You've just had three days off. School is your job and not one you can be lazy about. You've had plenty of sleep, so get up, lazybones." She opened the blinds, and sun streamed into the room.

Michael grumbled as he dressed and made his way to the kitchen. He didn't finish his cereal and fussed when it got too soggy. He drank his juice and moved slowly toward the door.

"Bye, Mom," he said in a glum voice, his chin hanging down to his chest.

"Bye, honey. I love you."

"Me too," he mumbled in the same glum voice, but his mom didn't pay any attention.

Michael and Jason made it to the bus and school without a problem and walked down the hallway toward their classrooms. They felt safe until loud footsteps slapped the floor behind them. Turning, they saw Chuck racing up to them.

"Hey, Chung King! Ya miss me?" His eyes danced, and he laughed loudly.

Michael and Jason didn't say anything and kept walking.

"I'll catch up with you after school, okay?" Chuck wagged his finger at them as he skipped backward toward his classroom.

"You should tell on him, Michael."

"Yeah, maybe."

Chapter 6

Trouble in School

Michael couldn't concentrate in class. He messed up on the directions for a worksheet and made several mistakes. When he tried to erase them, his paper tore. Now it was a mess. He bowed his head, shielding his eyes with his hand. Using his elbow to hold the paper in place, he tried to erase another error, tearing the sheet more and making a bigger mess.

It's no use; I'm gonna get marked down on this for sure. He put his pencil down and slouched back in his seat. *Anyway, what did Chuck mean by, "I'll catch you after school"?* His heart pounded. *Is he going to chase me again or what?* Michael raised his hand.

"Yes, Michael?"

"I don't feel good, Mrs. Ballou. Can I go see the nurse?"

"Why, of course. But I want someone to go with you." She looked around the classroom. "Andy, will you walk Michael down to the nurse's office, please?" She looked back at Michael, her brow furrowed. "Andy can carry your backpack for you. I hope you feel better soon, Michael."

"Thanks."

At the nurse's office, Andy handed him his backpack. "Sorry you're sick."

"Yeah, me too."

Michael sat in a chair. A minute later, the nurse came out of the back room and smiled at Michael.

"Hi, Ms. Jeanne."

"Hi there. I understand you aren't feeling well?"

"It's my stomach—and my head. I don't feel good."

"Well, we can't have that now, can we? Let's take your temperature and go from there." She stuck a thermometer in his ear. When it beeped, she looked at it. "Good, this says you don't have a temp. So let's go in the back room where you can lie down on one of my comfy cots. I'll get a cold compress for your head. Think that might help?"

"Maybe—"

"You just close your eyes and try to relax." She pulled a blanket up over him and patted his shoulder. "Have you had anything to eat today?"

"Yeah, I ate my lunch."

"Good. Was there anything you ate that might have made you feel sick?"

"No. I just feel sick."

"Okay, Michael, well, you just lie here and rest awhile. If you don't feel better in a little bit, we'll give your mom a call. Okay?"

Michael lay down on the cot and kept the compress over his eyes and forehead. He didn't want anyone to look at him. If they did, they'd see what a big chicken he was. He just wanted his mom to pick him up and take him home.

When the compress got warm, Ms. Jeanne gave him a fresh one. "Feel any better, Michael?"

"Not really."

"I'm sorry, hon. Let me give your mom a call."

Michael felt better already.

"I'm sorry, Michael; your mom didn't answer the phone, so I left a message. Should we call your dad, or do you think you can tough it out for another hour until school's out?"

"No, it'll take an hour for my dad to get here. I'll just stay here on the cot."

"Okay, but let me know if you feel any worse. You don't have a temperature, so maybe you've picked up a little bug."

"Yeah, probably." Michael wished he'd caught something. *I couldn't feel any worse without dying.*

When the dismissal bell rang, Michael got up slowly and picked up his backpack.

"Are you going to be okay, Michael?" Ms. Jeanne felt his forehead. "Should I get someone to walk with you?"

"Nah, I'm okay now, Ms. Jeanne. I'll ride home with Jason."

"Maybe you'll feel better after a little dinner and a good night's sleep. Sometimes after a long weekend we feel a little punk when we go back on our regular schedule."

"Yeah, thanks." Michael shuffled his feet and edged toward the door. He couldn't wait to get home. "Bye."

Michael left the building by the side entrance to avoid seeing Chuck and walked the long way around to the bus stop.

"What happened, Michael?" Jason demanded. "I looked all over for you, and then Mrs. Ballou said you'd gone to the nurse's office."

"I just had a stomachache."

"Oh, is that all! Well, let's get going, or Mrs. Murphy will leave without us."

The boys clambered aboard the bus, but their favorite seats behind the driver were taken, and they had to sit halfway down the aisle.

"How come you didn't save our seats, Eddie?"

"Hey, sorry, Jason. I did, but after a while I figured you guys weren't coming."

Michael was worried. *We won't be able to get out fast from these seats, and Chuck will have plenty of time to sneak around and hide before we get off.*

At their stop, Michael kept his eyes on Chuck as he and Jason made their way to the front of the bus. "Chuck's watching us, Jason. He's going out the rear door. We gotta hurry."

"Bye, Mrs. Murphy."

"You boys take care," she called out.

The bus pulled away from the curb, leaving them alone on the sidewalk. But Chuck's friends had gone on without him.

"What's he doing?" Jason whispered.

"Just watching us."

"Let's run."

They kept turning back to see what Chuck was up to, but Chuck was just following them, walking slowly.

"Think he's trying to find out where we live?" asked Michael.

"Yeah, so he'll know where our fort is."

"We can't let him find out.

Jason looked back. "He's still following us, Michael."

"Just keep running. We'll go past my house; then I'll cut through Mrs. Leslie's yard and circle back to my house. He'll think *her* house is mine. You run past your house and do the same thing."

"Yeah, so he won't know where either of us lives." Jason laughed. "That's a great plan. Call me when you get home."

"Okay."

Michael sneaked in through the back door of his house. He was pretty sure that Chuck had not seen him. "Yesss," he said aloud, pumping his fist.

"I'm home, Mom!"

"Hi, honey! Are you okay? I dashed to the store, and when I got home, I found a message from the school nurse. What happened?"

"Awww, nothing, really. I'm okay. Just had a stomachache, but it's gone now."

"You look flushed."

"That's from running."

"Maybe you shouldn't be gulping down orange juice if you have a stomachache."

"Mom, it's gone. I'm okay! Besides, I've gotta call Jason."

——————◄o►——————

At dinner, Mom served him chicken rice soup. She said she didn't want him getting another stomachache. Michael felt guilty about saying he was sick. *I did have a headache, but maybe it wasn't bad enough to call my mom to come get me.*

The telephone rang, and Michael jumped. The spoon flew out of his hand and dropped on the table.

"I'll get it, Michael," his dad said. "I'm expecting a call."

If it's a hang-up call, it's probably Chuck. He'd be too chicken to say Chung King to Dad. Michael listened carefully.

"My son? Are you sure? Well, certainly! Yes, I'll have a talk with him. Of course. I'll get back to you as soon as we've straightened this out. Thank you for calling."

Dad returned to the table frowning and slowly put his napkin back on his lap. He pursed his lips and glanced across the table at Michael's mom.

"What is it, Matt?" Mom asked.

"That call was from our neighbor, Mrs. Leslie." He looked at Michael. "Is there anything you want to tell your mother and me?"

Michael shook his head. "Ummm, no."

"Think harder."

Geez, he's really getting mad. Why's he looking at me *like that?* "I really don't."

"You have no idea why Mrs. Leslie might be calling me?"

"Huh? No, I don't."

"Mrs. Leslie says you were in her backyard this afternoon, and you trampled all the flowers in her garden."

"Huh? No, I didn't."

Michael is seen sneaking through Mrs. Leslie's yard

"She says she *saw* you in her backyard."

"Yeah, but I didn't mess up her flowers. Honest."

"What were you doing in her backyard, Michael?" Mom was looking upset now too. "Didn't you come straight home from the bus?"

"I took a shortcut."

"A shortcut!" Dad threw his arms up in the air. "She lives farther away from the bus than we do!"

"But I was walking with Jason and went too far, and I had to cut back."

"Through backyards? Was Jason with you?"

"Yes—I mean, no! I mean, he went on home, and I cut through the back."

"So you were the only one in Mrs. Leslie's yard?"

"Yeah, but—" Michael stammered.

"Obviously, you weren't careful if you trampled her flowers. After dinner we'll call Mrs. Leslie. You'll apologize and tell her you'll be over on Saturday to make things right."

"But Dad—"

"No buts, Michael. You'll tell her that you'll clean up her garden and replant her flowers. Also, you can ask if there's anything else she'd like done around her yard. There'll be no working on the fort until Mrs. Leslie is satisfied."

Michael hung his head. Dad's mind was made up!

"I'm very disappointed," Mom began.

"But it wasn't me, Mom!"

"Then how did Mrs. Leslie *see* you?" His dad was still sputtering. "From now on, I don't want you taking *shortcuts* through anybody's yard. Yards are private property, Michael; I've taught you that."

Michael slumped in the chair and crossed his arms over his chest. *There weren't any dumb old flowers behind the bushes—just dirt. I know 'cause I was crawling in it to stay down low so Chuck wouldn't see me. Chuck! That's who did it. He thought it was* my *house. Oh, great!*

Michael looked first at Mom and then at Dad. They were *still* scowling. *I'm not gonna open my mouth, 'cause they'll just get mad all over again. What would I tell 'em, anyway?* He sighed and shrugged his shoulders. "Sorry."

"Sorry doesn't help. You just can't go around damaging other people's property." Dad was still shaking his head.

Gosh, I said I was sorry for something I didn't even do. If I tell on Chuck now, he's gonna get even madder. But if I don't, they'll keep blaming me. Why'd that stupid Chuck have to mess up Mrs. Leslie's garden, anyway? Wait 'til I tell Jason!

Michael made the call to Mrs. Leslie. She sounded disappointed about losing her flowers but didn't yell or anything, probably because Dad said Michael would fix everything on Saturday. Plus, if Michael did a good job and mowed the back lawn too, she said she'd forget about what happened.

Great! Chuck gets away with being a rat, and I do all the work. Plus, I'm the one who has to keep apologizing to everyone.

At bedtime, Michael hurried up to his room and got ready for bed, glad to get away by himself. Grabbing his baseball mitt and glove, he flopped down on the bed, crossed his legs, and slapped the ball into the glove several times. He tossed it up in the air and caught it. Smack. Over and over the ball went up and then smacked back into his glove. *How'd I get into this mess, anyway? We only wanted to keep the fort a secret from Chuck. He's ruined everything.*

"Time to put up your glove and get some sleep, sport," Dad said from the doorway. "I can understand you're probably feeling bad about today, but you'll feel better once everything is straightened out with Mrs. Leslie on Saturday. Now get some sleep."

Mom came into the bedroom and put some laundry on the dresser. She smiled at him. "You'll feel better once you've repaired the garden. You're a good boy, Michael. You just did something wrong. Fortunately, it's something that you can fix." She kissed him on the forehead. "I love you. Sleep tight."

Okay! I've heard that a hundred times now. I said I'm gonna fix it, even though I didn't do it! Out loud he said, "I'm really sorry. I'll make Mrs. Leslie's garden look great again." *Mrs. Leslie musta thought Chuck was me. But, hey, at least Chuck doesn't know where our fort is!*

Dad patted his head and kissed him good night on the forehead. "Sleep tight."

At least they aren't still acting all ugly and mad about everything 'cause I'm accepting responsibility. Hah!

The next morning, the second he saw Jason coming down the street, Michael raced out. "Wait 'til you hear what Chuck did!"

"What?"

"Well, you know how I ducked down behind Mrs. Leslie's house?"

"Yeah?"

"Well, Chuck really thinks I live there, and when he couldn't find our fort, he messed up all Mrs. Leslie's flowers. Then Mrs. Leslie called my dad and said *I* did it, because she saw *me* sneaking through her yard."

"You're kidding. Did you tell your dad?"

"I tried, but he didn't believe me because of what Mrs. Leslie said."

"Wait! Did you tell him *everything*?" Jason demanded. "Even about Chuck?"

"I kept trying, but he wouldn't even listen. He got really mad and kept saying I'd done it 'cause Mrs. Leslie said so."

"But you didn't, so you gotta tell him about Chuck."

"Yeah, and then what? He'll think I was a jerk for getting mad about a stupid old name. And you know what else? We can't work on the fort Saturday 'cause I've gotta fix Mrs. Leslie's garden."

"I kept telling you to tell somebody, but you wouldn't." Jason punched Michael's arm. "Now what're you gonna do?"

Chapter 7

Jason Spills the Beans

Michael kept glancing at the clock on the wall behind Mrs. Ballou's desk. *Will it ever ring? What a lousy week. Chuck keeps teasing me and trying to scare me. He found out I was sneaking out the side door to get to the bus, so he went out early and blocked the door. I had to go all the way back around again. If Jason hadn't asked Mrs. Murphy to wait one more minute, I'd have missed the bus. I'm so glad it's Friday.*

The bell rang, and Michael raced out to find Jason.

"Let's wait by the bus monitor like we used to." Michael ran ahead toward their bus. However, the bus was already at the curb waiting, and kids were already getting on it.

"Hey, Mrs. Murphy!" Michael was happy Eddie had saved their seats.

"Hey, boys. You certainly look happy it's Friday."

"We are," they answered.

Michael didn't see Chuck on the bus. "Hey, Jason, did ya notice Chuck's not here?"

"He isn't?" Jason stood and checked the back of the bus. "I wonder where he is? Do you think he's hiding?"

"No, I never saw him get on."

"What are you boys up to?" Mrs. Murphy eyed them in her rearview mirror.

"Oh, nothing," they answered together.

"Maybe you and I should have a little talk when we get to your stop."

"What does she want to talk to us about?" Jason whispered.

Michael scowled. "Did you tell anyone about me and Chuck?"

"Only about him messing up the flowers. But I only told *one* kid in my class, and he doesn't even ride our bus."

"Oh, great. Who'd you tell?"

"Just Robby. He's cool."

"Robby!" wailed Michael. "Not him! Robby's big brother Josh is in the same class as Chuck. I'm dog meat!"

"No, you're not," insisted Jason. "Josh's in sixth grade."

"Yeah, and so is Chuck!"

"Gosh, I'm sorry, Michael. I didn't even think about that. I was just mad about what Chuck did, so I made Robby promise not to tell any more kids about the fort. Do you think he'll tell Josh? Hey, maybe he won't say anything."

"Yeah, right!" Michael slumped down in his seat. "Chuck is gonna be really mad when he finds out I tricked him."

"You mad at me, Michael?" Jason asked, seeing the sullen look on Michael's face. "I'm real sorry. Maybe we could call Robby and tell him not to tell his brother."

"Nah. It's too late. I just wish we hadn't said anything to anybody." Michael swallowed hard to keep from crying.

"I'm really sorry. It was kinda fun tricking Chuck, but maybe it won't be so good once Chuck finds out, huh?"

The school bus rumbled up Michael's street and squealed to a stop. The doors hissed open, and a group of noisy children tumbled out.

Michael and Jason stayed slumped in their seats waiting to see why Mrs. Murphy wanted to talk to them.

Once the bus was empty, Mrs. Murphy shut off the engine, got out of her seat, and sat opposite Michael and Jason. She glanced from one boy to the other. "I'd like you boys to tell me about Chuck."

"Chuck?" Michael gulped some air and started coughing.

"What do you mean?" Jason looked at Michael.

"I'd like to know about Chuck," she said kindly.

"Tell her, Michael," whispered Jason.

"Tell me what, Michael?" Mrs. Murphy prodded him in a gentle voice.

Michael stared at his shoes.

"Come on, Michael; look at me. I don't want you to be afraid to talk to me. I know something is bothering you."

"Do it, Michael!" Jason gave him a nudge.

Michael looked up at Mrs. Murphy. "Ummm—" He swallowed hard and started again. "Well, ummm, I tricked Chuck into thinking I lived in a different house, and he ripped up the flowers there. But it wasn't my house, so he tore up Mrs. Leslie's flowers, and now I'm the one being punished."

"Yeah!" Jason nodded. "It was all Chuck's fault."

"Whoa. Let's go back and start from the beginning." Mrs. Murphy adjusted herself in the small seat. "Can you think of what started the problems between you and Chuck?"

Once Michael started telling Mrs. Murphy the story, *everything* seemed to bubble up and out of his mouth. "I hate being called Chung King, and I hate being scared of Chuck. When I dropped my backpack, he messed it all up. He threw my papers all over the street, and I had to pick them up. I tried sneaking out of the school so Chuck wouldn't see me. Then he called me at home and called me Chung King on the telephone." Michael stopped to catch his breath.

"We've been waiting by the school monitor so he couldn't bug us," added Jason.

"And I don't want to go to the bus stop unless Jason's there. Then when Chuck found out about our fort, he tried to follow us home. We tricked him and went the wrong way. I ducked through Mrs. Leslie's yard so he'd think I lived in her house. And it worked, but then he went there and tore up the flowers. Mrs. Leslie didn't see Chuck in her yard, but she saw me and thought I messed up the flowers. So she told my dad, and now my mom and dad think I disrespected Mrs. Leslie's property." When Michael got to the end, his chest heaved and tears spilled down his cheeks.

Jason put his arm around Michael's shoulder. "It's okay, Michael."

Mrs. Murphy patted his arm. "Have you spoken to your parents about this, Michael?"

"Nooo. Well, I tried, but they didn't understand." Michael wiped his tears on his sleeve.

"I wish you had come to me. I would never let anyone bully you like this."

Michael sniffed. "Bully me? But he didn't. It's only name-calling, and now they're going to say I'm a tattletale."

Mrs. Murphy got a tissue for him and sat back down. "Michael, this was more than just name-calling. You've been too frightened to go to the bus alone, and you haven't felt safe at school. This is wrong, and I'm sorry this happened."

"But you can't tell Chuck I told. He'll just get madder at me," begged Michael.

"Or at me." Jason's eyes flashed wide open.

"Boys, you'll be okay. This kind of behavior is a problem for adults to handle. We'll make sure no one retaliates against you or anyone else if they report this kind of behavior."

"How?" Michael blew his nose.

"You let me take care of it over the weekend. Monday morning I want to see happy faces at the bus stop." Mrs. Murphy smiled at them. "Thank you, Jason, for encouraging Michael to talk to me. You're a good friend."

"Thanks, Mrs. Murphy." Michael wiped his face on his sleeve.

"Oh, one more thing, Michael: I want you to talk to your mom and dad. They need to know that you had a problem and that you did the right thing by talking to me. Tell them that someone from school will call them about it this evening."

"Okay." Michael gave Mrs. Murphy a hug. "Thanks a lot! Come on, Jason."

As Michael and Jason went down the steps, they looked both ways to see if Chuck was waiting for them. He wasn't, so they took their time walking home.

"You okay, Michael?"

"*No!* Now I have to tell my parents."

"But that's a good thing," insisted Jason.

"I guess." Michael jumped over a crack in the sidewalk.

"Now you won't have to fix Mrs. Leslie's garden, and we can work on the fort."

"Maybe, but what if Chuck lies and says I did it?"

Chapter 8

False Accusations

Michael finished the last bite of dinner and took a sip of milk. He swallowed and cleared his throat. Dad had frowned through dinner and Mom had been very quiet, so he knew they were still upset with him. His heart skipped wildly.

"Ummm, Mom, Dad, I've got something to tell you." His hands felt clammy as he clasped them together under the table.

"Go ahead, Michael." His dad put down his fork and leaned forward, giving Michael his full attention.

"Ummm, today on the way home from school, Mrs. Murphy wanted to talk to me and Jason."

"Jason and me," corrected his mother.

"Yeah, Jason and me," repeated Michael.

His dad's eyes narrowed. "What were you doing?"

"No, Dad!" Michael held up his hand. "Nothing like that. It was 'cause of this kid on the bus that's been scaring us and calling me names. He's the one that messed up Mrs. Leslie's flowers. I didn't tell you because I thought you'd think I was a baby for getting mad about name-calling. But Mrs. Murphy said that name-calling is part of bullying, and bullying isn't allowed on the bus or at school."

"What are you saying, Michael? That you didn't trample Mrs. Leslie's flowers?" His mom's eyebrow arched.

"Right."

"Then why didn't you just say so?"

"I did."

"Let's start over—from the beginning." Dad rubbed his forehead. "Who is Chuck, and what's he got to do with this?"

Michael went over the whole story, just as he had with Mrs. Murphy. "And Mrs. Murphy or somebody from school is gonna call you about it tonight."

Michael thought he was in the clear until he saw the funny looks his parents gave each other and saw his mom shake her head and look into her lap.

"I still don't understand why you let us go on believing you ruined Mrs. Leslie's flower bed. That kind of omission is almost like lying. Can you see that, Michael?"

"Yeah, Dad, I do now. But back then I was afraid of Chuck."

"I'm sorry I jumped to conclusions about Mrs. Leslie's garden, Michael." Dad looked intently into Michael's eyes. "But mostly I'm sorry you didn't think you could come to me about this guy, Chuck."

Michael shrugged.

"Well, tomorrow we'll go over to Mrs. Leslie's, and you can explain what happened. Then maybe you and I can help her out and replant the garden together. Perhaps afterward we'll still have some time to work on the fort."

"Great, thanks, Dad."

"Michael, we're your parents. You can talk to us about anything." Mom reached over and squeezed his hand.

"Yeah, I know." Michael squirmed. His legs were tired from sitting.

Dad's fingers tapped the table. "And if you have a problem, tiger, we want to know about it. I never would have tolerated anyone bullying you! Understand?"

"Yeah, I really do. Can I call Jason now and tell him we can work on the fort tomorrow?"

His dad smiled. "Better wait until we see how long we'll be at Mrs. Leslie's."

The telephone rang, and Michael smiled. It was probably Mrs. Murphy calling to say he hadn't done anything wrong. Yesss! Boy, it felt good not to have his parents mad at him anymore. He tried to listen to his dad's side of the conversation.

"Yes, Mr. Watt, I'm glad you called. Michael just filled us in on what's been going on. You know how kids are. Yes, sir, he kept it to himself. We had no idea he was having any problems. If we'd known, we'd have contacted Mrs. Ballou or you. Thank you for taking care of everything. Good night."

A big load seemed to lift from Michael's shoulders. He was happy Jason had bugged him to tell Mrs. Murphy and that Mrs. Murphy had told the principal. *That'll take care of Chuck. And after tomorrow, Mrs. Leslie won't be mad at me either.* He couldn't stop grinning.

Michael woke up on Saturday morning before his parents. He lay in bed thinking about everything that had happened and chuckled about what probably had happened at Chuck's house last night. *I'll bet he got restricted to his yard. No, maybe to his room, and maybe he'll have it for a month.* Michael laughed out loud. *Yeah, Chuck's in his room with no TV privileges, eating bread and water, and peeing in a jar. I wish I could be a bug on the wall. I wonder if old toughie cried when the principal told his parents? Yes! This is gonna be a great day!*

After breakfast, Michael and his dad filled a small wheelbarrow with garden tools and wheeled it up to Mrs. Leslie's house.

"Go ahead, Michael. Ring the bell. See if Mrs. Leslie has a minute to talk before we start to work."

Michael pushed the button and heard the *ding-dong* of the bell. He shoved his hands in his pockets and waited.

Mrs. Leslie opened the door and smiled. "I'm sorry I took so long; I was on the phone."

"Mrs. Leslie, I need to explain something to you."

"Of course, dear."

Michael began his story and got to the part where Chuck had trampled her garden.

"Oh goodness, no!" Mrs. Leslie's hand flew to her mouth. "He didn't ruin my flowers."

"Huh?" Michael was stunned by her reaction.

"No, honey, it wasn't you or any of your friends. I know that now."

"Huh?" was all Michael could say.

Michael's dad interrupted, "Excuse me. Mrs. Leslie, you say it wasn't one of the boys who trampled your flowers?"

"That's right. I was just on the phone explaining everything to Mrs. Kim. I feel so bad about accusing your son." She looked at Michael.

"So you know it was Chuck who did it?" Michael was still confused.

"Oh no, dear! That's what I'm trying to say. None of you boys did it. It was my daughter's big old bulldog, Jackson. Hope was staying here while I was away, and she decided it would be a good time to give Jackson a bath. The minute she finished toweling him off, he raced around the yard and rolled all over my beautiful flowers. She left a message for me on my computer, but I didn't see it. When I got home, I happened to see you crawling out by the back fence. Later when I saw my garden, I assumed you were the one who did the damage. I didn't know any better until Hope called today. I'm very sorry I accused you wrongly, Michael."

Who ruined the flower bed?

"Wow, so it was Jackson!" Michael laughed.

"I'm not so sure this is a laughing matter, Michael."
Dad was shaking his head again.

"I mean, I'm sorry about your flowers and all.
I'm just laughing because it's great I'm not in trouble
for it."

"Hmmm. Your troubles aren't over yet." Dad put a hand on Michael's shoulder. "There's another party who's been falsely accused of trampling Mrs. Leslie's garden."

Michael's eyes rolled back in his head. *"Chuck!"*

———◄O►———

Chapter 9

Making Things Right

Michael was confused. A minute ago nobody was mad at him. Problems solved. *Now here I am back in trouble! And by tonight, a lot of people are gonna be mad at me again. Especially Chuck! What if his parents got really mad at him and made him stay in his room all night, or I made him miss a movie or kept him from going to the skateboard park, or—agggh. Jeepers, Chuck's going to make me pay for this!*

"Michael." Dad interrupted his thoughts. "What do you think we should do about this situation?"

"I don't know." Michael shrugged his shoulders. "Maybe you could call his dad or something?"

Dad frowned. "No, I don't think that would do it. You've damaged Chuck's reputation and—"

"But Dad, he's been picking on me and calling me names and doing all kinds of things."

"Yes, and that's being taken care of. I'm talking about what *you* did, not what Chuck did."

Michael slumped in the chair and hung his head. "What should I do, Dad?"

"Make it right. Speak to all the people who think Chuck trampled Mrs. Leslie's flowers because of what you told them. Set them straight."

"Oh no! I have to call Mr. Watt?"

"Yes."

"And Mrs. Murphy?"

"Yes. Everyone, including your friends."

Michael's stomach churned. *They're gonna think I'm such a jerk. I hate Chuck. This wouldn't have happened if he hadn't started it.*

"Let's get going." His dad motioned for him to come to the phone. "I know this is tough, son. But the sooner you get it over with, the better you'll feel. I'll look up the numbers and help you make the calls."

Michael's hands were sweaty as he grasped the receiver.

"Who are we calling first?"

"Mr. Watt. You ready?"

Dialing the number, Michael prayed he'd get a recorder.

"Hello."

The words stuck in Michael's throat. "Ummm, ah—"

"Yes, who is this?"

"Ummm, Michael Kim, Mr. Watt."

"Yes, hello, Michael. I'm glad to hear from you. I spoke with your dad last night. Has he spoken to you? I want you to know that I'm taking care of everything."

"Yes, and that's why I had to call—" Michael's mouth went dry. "There's something else—"

"Something else?"

"Well, Chuck didn't tear up Mrs. Leslie's garden. It was her daughter's bulldog who did it." Michael took a deep breath. *There, I said it.*

"What was that?" Mr. Watt sputtered. "Chuck didn't destroy—but you told me—and I—"

"I know, but I made a big mistake, and I'm really sorry. Here's my dad." Michael shoved the phone into his dad's hand.

"Mr. Watt, it seems there was a rush to judgment on Michael's part about Chuck's involvement with Mrs. Leslie's garden."

They seemed to talk forever. Michael dreaded whatever they were dreaming up for him. *Watch, I'll be the one restricted to my room for a year, eating bread and water and peeing in a jug!*

Dad hung up. "That was good, Michael. Mr. Watt wants to call Chuck's parents first, so we'll call the next person on your list. Who's next?"

Great! I don't have to talk to pig head! "Ummm, Mrs. Murphy."

Michael repeated his story, telling Mrs. Murphy exactly what he'd told Mr. Watt.

"No, I'm not angry with you, Michael, but I am disappointed. It means that what I said to Mr. Watt and Mrs. Ballou wasn't true."

"Oh no! You told Mrs. Ballou?"

"Yes, Michael, and she contacted Chuck's teacher. The three of us met with Mr. Watt this morning. We want to put an end to bullying. It's part of our job."

Michael groaned. "Here's my dad, Mrs. Murphy."

By the time Michael finished the calls, he was tired and hungry. He stood up and headed toward the kitchen.

"Not so fast, Michael. You have one more call to make."

"Who?"

"Chuck."

"Ah gee, Dad, he hates me. Do I hafta? Besides, you said Mr. Watt was gonna call his parents."

"You owe him an explanation."

It just didn't seem fair to Michael. *Why can't* you *talk to him? Yeah, why can't* you *tell him what a rat he is, and to stop picking on me and Jason!*

"The longer you wait, the tougher it will be." Dad patted Michael's head and handed him the phone. "Come on, sport. Here's the number."

Michael took his time punching in the numbers. A lady answered the phone.

"Hello, I'm Michael Kim—"

"Hello, Michael. Hold on, and let me get Chuck."

"Yeah," Chuck answered.

"This is Michael."

"Oh yeah, Chung King."

"No, Michael!"

Chuck snickered. "That really bugs you, doesn't it?"

"Well, it's not my name. It's a Chinese name."

Chuck just laughed. "So why ya calling?"

"'Cause I thought you were the one who ruined Mrs. Leslie's flower bed, and I told Mrs. Murphy, and she told Mrs. Ballou, and Mrs. Ballou told your teacher, and they all told Mr. Watt."

"Yeah, but I didn't do it."

"I know, but I thought you did it." Michael's hand shook as he spoke into the phone.

"Why?" Chuck asked.

"To get me in trouble since I didn't show you our fort."

"Nah, and besides, my mom knew it wasn't me because she took me to the dentist and we were there all afternoon."

"So you didn't get in trouble?"

"Nah. Not for that."

"Whew." Michael let out his breath. This was better than he'd expected.

"Mom told Mr. Watt I didn't do it, but you still got me in trouble. Now my parents and me hafta go to school for a meeting with Mr. Watt."

Michael didn't say anything.

"You still there, Chung King?"

"Yeah."

"So what else did you say about me?"

"I don't kn-know," stammered Michael.

"Well, you'd better remember by the time I see you at the bus stop!"

The phone went dead.

Chapter 10

Will Dad Help Me?

At bedtime, Michael's dad came into his room and sat on the edge of the bed.

"I'm very proud of you for making those calls. I know it wasn't easy."

"Thanks, Dad, but I'm kinda scared of seeing Chuck at the bus stop."

"I know, son, but don't worry about Monday. Mom and I are driving you to school; and Chuck's parents will be driving him. Mr. Watt has arranged a meeting for everyone involved, including Mrs. Murphy and your teachers. We're going to iron out this problem with Chuck once and for all."

"Really? That's great, Dad!" Michael gulped. "I didn't think you were going to help me."

His dad grabbed him in a bear hug. "You don't think I'd let some punk keep bullying you, do you?" He drew back and looked deep into Michael's eyes.

"We all make mistakes, but it's what we do *afterward* that counts."

Michael wiped his eyes with the back of his hand.

"If you'd let Chuck take the blame for the flowers, then your actions would have been just as bad as Chuck's. But you did the right thing." He tickled Michael's tummy. "You're a great kid, and I want you to stay that way."

"Thanks, Dad."

————◀o▶————

On Saturday, Michael and his dad didn't get to work on the fort. Mrs. Leslie's garden took longer than expected, but Michael had fun working alongside his dad. Mrs. Leslie made them lunch, and they sat on the grass and talked about a lot of things, like what it was like when his dad was a kid and what happened when *he* got in trouble. Michael felt better than he had for a long time. *I just hope everyone can keep Chuck away from me!*

Jason and his dad came over after church on Sunday. Michael and Mr. Lewis attached the shutters to the window frames, and Jason and Mr. Kim put the Dutch door on to the door frame. The boys used rollers to paint the outside walls white, while Mr. Lewis was on the roof spray-painting the railings a bright red. Mr. Kim tackled the door using a brush to paint it navy blue.

When the floor was finished, they all put their brushes and rollers in a pail of soapy water and rolled up the tarps they'd used to protect the grass from getting covered with paint.

"Wow, Michael, this is the best fort ever built!" Jason threw up his hand and gave Michael a high five.

"Yeah, I can't wait until the paint dries!"

At bedtime, Michael was tired from all the work he'd done but couldn't go to sleep. He tossed and turned and kept adjusting his pillow. *What's everyone gonna say at the meeting tomorrow? What if Chuck lies about being mean to me or about calling me names? What if he decides to be mean because I said he'd torn up the flowers? I wish I could go to a different school.*

The fort

Chapter 11

Reaching an Understanding

Michael and his parents arrived right on time at Federal Street Elementary School, but Principal Watt was already in a meeting with Chuck and his parents. The secretary asked the Kim family to take seats and wait.

I wonder what Chuck's saying in there? He's probably blaming everything on me, but he was a jerk first. Michael twitched in his seat. *But I don't care as long as they make him stop picking on me. What if he doesn't? What if he just gets sneakier? Why are they taking so long?*

The door to the conference room opened, and Mr. Watt smiled and motioned for Michael to come in.

"Hello, Michael, Mr. and Mrs. Kim. Please come in, and I'll introduce everyone."

Michael sat down between his parents, being careful not to look at Chuck.

When Chuck was introduced, he shook hands with Michael's parents. So when it was Michael's turn, he shook hands with Chuck's parents.

Chuck's acting all nicey-nice because all the adults are here, but they don't know how he is in school.

Mr. Watt continued, "I believe you boys need no introduction."

Michael and Chuck nodded their heads.

There was a tap on the conference room door, and Michael and Chuck's teachers walked in and sat down.

"I've called this meeting today," Mr. Watt began, "because I have a problem and I need some help solving it." He looked at Chuck's parents and then at Michael's. "I spoke with Chuck this morning, and he and his parents were concerned about Chuck being falsely accused of destroying Mrs. Leslie's flower bed."

"But Mr. Watt," Michael interrupted, raising his hand.

"Michael, you'll have your turn. Please wait."

Michael slumped in his chair and looked at Chuck, who was looking at Mr. Watt.

"But they appreciate that you called everyone involved to correct your mistake, Michael."

Michael's mom patted his knee under the table.

"I've discussed something with Chuck that has to do with you, Michael. You've been having a problem but didn't tell anyone about it except Mrs. Murphy—and that was only recently. Is that right?"

Michael sat up straight in his chair and stole a glance at Chuck. Chuck was fiddling with at his hands in his lap. "Yes, sir," Michael said in a voice just above a whisper.

"Did you feel that Chuck was having some fun with you?"

"No, sir."

"Did you think he was just teasing?"

"No, sir."

"Were you afraid of him?"

"Yes, sir."

"But I wasn't—" Chuck protested.

Mr. Watt put his hand up to silence him. "Chuck, please wait your turn." The chair screeched as Mr. Watt stood up. "Do you see my problem, boys? One of you says he was just having fun. The other says it wasn't fun at all. One of you got hurt but didn't think it was important enough to report. Someone else wrongly accused someone, which hurt someone else." He rubbed the back of his neck. "It seems the problem is that nobody knows what is fun and what isn't. Or that if they don't stop doing something, especially after being asked—well, we call that *bullying*. That's right, *bullying*."

Everyone in the room watched Mr. Watt as he paced back and forth talking and rubbing the back of his neck. "Now, how do you suppose I'm going to handle this problem? Michael, do you have an idea about this?"

"Well, I don't like being called Chung King; I told Chuck that a hundred times, and he just kept on doing it." Michael sucked in a big breath.

"Chuck?" Mr. Watt nodded at him.

"It was just a funny name, Michael. I was trying to be funny like sometimes when people call me Woodchuck-chuck."

"Did you like it when they called you that?" Michael looked Chuck in the eye.

Chuck shrugged. "Not really."

"Then don't call me Chung King. I'm not Chinese, ya know."

"How would I know?" Chuck rolled his eyes. "I just thought it was a neat name, and you kinda reminded me of that little Chung King kid on TV."

"Once you know someone doesn't like a name, you need to stop using it." Chuck's teacher was looking at him. "It might be amusing to you, but to others, name-calling can be hurtful. Is there anything you want to say to Michael?" his teacher asked.

"Yeah, I'm sorry, and I won't call you that anymore."

"Okay." Michael looked at Chuck. *He probably doesn't mean that.*

Mrs. Ballou cocked her head and looked at Michael. "What else has been bothering you, Michael?"

"Another thing is—I don't like it when he won't let us through a door or when he jumps out from behind the bus or bushes and scares us."

"I guess I shouldn't do that either." Chuck laughed and raised his eyebrows. "But Michael, you shoulda seen your face! You were *great*! Your arms and legs kinda flew out in different directions. It was so funny, and you jumped three feet off the ground! Honest!"

Michael almost laughed at the picture Chuck painted of him but stopped himself. "Yeah, it probably was funny for *you*, but then you kept on doing it, and I got scared."

"Are you beginning to see the line between fun and not fun?" Mr. Watt asked Chuck.

"Yeah, only do something to somebody once?"

"Not exactly."

"Were you really afraid of me, Michael?" Chuck asked. "It's not like I pretended to hit you or tried to trip you or hurt you or anything. Know what I mean? I'm sorry, though."

"And there's another thing." Michael looked at Mr. Watt to be sure he was listening. "What about my backpack?" He turned back to Chuck. "You dumped it all over the street."

"Huh? No, I didn't. You dropped it in the middle of the street and just left it there. A car came by and hit it and the papers flew all over. But I got it and put it on the sidewalk by the lamppost so it wouldn't get run over again. I didn't know where your house was, but I figured you'd come back for it."

"Gosh. I didn't know." Michael's face flushed. "Sorry about that—and I'm sorry about telling everybody you messed up Mrs. Leslie's garden. I really thought you were trying to get me in trouble."

"Nah, my parents would put me on restriction for a year for something like that."

"You're right about that, son." Chuck's dad looked at Michael. "We hope Chuck knows better now. I don't mean to excuse his behavior, but maybe if I tell you a little about our family, you'll see where Chuck was coming from. He was behaving like his three older brothers who are always playing tricks on him." He looked at Chuck. "The difference is that Chuck has the advantage of knowing his brothers aren't going to hurt him. If they go too far, he knows we'll put a stop to it." Frowning, he went on. "Unfortunately, Michael, you had no way of knowing you weren't going to be hurt, and I can understand you being frightened and worried you would be."

Michael's mouth fell open as he stared at Chuck. "Your brothers scare you like that?"

"Oh yeah—and worse! We all try to get each other, but Mom hates it, so we can't do it when she's around." Chuck looked at his mom and wrinkled his nose.

"Because someone always goes too far," Mrs. Howard added.

"Now you know it's inappropriate with anyone other than your brothers." Mr. Howard wagged his finger at him. "I hope you both learned something today. Maybe now you both can work on putting the bad feelings behind you?"

Chuck looked at Michael. "I can if you can."

"I guess I can."

"Friends, then?" Chuck raised his hand and Michael slapped a high five on it.

"I gather you boys understand what went wrong between you and the behavior won't happen again?" Mr. Watt sat back down and leaned back in his chair. "Am I correct?"

"Yes, sir!"

"In that case, I'm canceling your detention. Instead, your parents have agreed to let you both work for me two days a week."

Michael and Chuck groaned.

"On Tuesdays and Thursdays, you boys will join me here in the conference room, along with your teachers and Mrs. Murphy. We're going to develop an important educational program for our school."

Michael and Chuck eyed each other.

"How can we do that?" Michael asked.

"Yeah, we're just kids," Chuck added.

"We need you to help us identify behavior that's in violation of the Student Anti-bully Code," Mr. Watt explained.

Chuck shrugged his shoulders. "I don't even know a Student Anti-bully Code."

"Me neither," said Michael.

Mr. Watt laughed. "That's right, boys, and that's our problem. We don't have one—*yet.* But we will have one soon because you boys are going to help us write it!"

Mr. Watt stood up. "Well, I think we've achieved what we came here for—meeting adjourned."

Michael wanted to talk to Mrs. Murphy. He still felt bad about telling her the wrong stuff. He gritted his teeth and went over to her. "I'm sorry I blamed Chuck for the flowers, Mrs. Murphy."

"Well, thanks for correcting your story. That was the right thing to do!" Mrs. Murphy gathered Michael in a hug. "Chuck, come on over here," she said, and gathered him into the hug too. "I can use your expertise. You guys are going to be my extra eyes and ears so that nothing like this *ever* happens again on *my* bus!"

"But isn't that like tattling?" Chuck asked, still confused.

"No. There's a big difference. Once we create the Student Anti-bully Code and the kids learn the rules, they'll be expected to follow them. If they break the rules, they'll be written up and will have to suffer the consequences of their actions."

The anti-bullying code of conduct

"So we'd report anyone breaking the rules to Mr. Watt, and then he'd talk to them like he did to us." Michael hugged Mrs. Murphy back.

"Yeah," Chuck said. "And maybe if someone thinks they're only teasing and they really aren't, we can get them to quit it before anyone gets hurt."

"Hey, Chuck, we can be like an anti-bullying team."

"Or how about the Anti-bullying Patrol?" Chuck's eyes danced.

Mr. Watt shook everyone's hand. "I'm pleased you boys have straightened things out between you. I'm also pleased that you'll be working with us to make this school a better place."

Michael raised his hands in the air. "Wait, everyone. There's one more important thing I forgot to tell you about." He kept a serious look on his face as he looked at Mr. Watt and then at Chuck.

The room went quiet.

Chuck's eyes opened wide in alarm. "What?"

"About our fort—would you like to see it?"

Everyone laughed, and Chuck chased a giggling Michael out of the conference room just as the bell rang for the beginning of classes.

---The End---

Questions and Answers

How difficult would it be to make a fort like Michael and Jason's?

Remember, a lot of supplies would have to be bought and carried home, unless you are lucky enough to find discarded items to use. Here are some of the materials Michael and Jason used:

- six sheets of plywood for the sides, roof, floor, and window cover
- bricks to protect the floor against wetness
- one used screen door
- twenty-two butterflies to screw the plywood pieces together
- eighty-eight screws for the butterflies
- four hinges: two for the front door and two for the push-up window covering
- two sets of hooks and eyes to hold the window cover open

- wood for making the railing and slats for a roof deck
- one roll of tarpaper for the roof to help keep the water out
- one used ladder in good condition to climb up to the roof deck
- an electric saw, an electric screwdriver, an electric nail gun, leftover paint and brushes, and a leftover piece of wood for the doorstep
- leftover paint

What do you remember? (Don't look at the answers first!)

1. What was the first thing Mr. Lewis and Jason did before putting the fort together?
2. What made it easier for Mr. Lee and Mr. Lewis to put the fort together?
3. What did Michael learn from Mr. Lee?
4. How did they use the bricks?
5. Why?
6. What was the tarpaper used for?
7. Could you make this fort without the ladder or roof deck on top?

8. What would you add to the fort to make it more fun for you?
9. Do you think building a fort like this would be fun or too much work?

Answers:

1. They cleared the land of rocks and sticks and made the dirt smooth.
2. Mr. Lee had precut all the wood pieces and marked where each piece of wood should be connected.
3. Michael learned how to start sawing by drawing *back* on the saw first, making a groove, and then pushing forward.
4. They arranged them in the dirt where the fort was to be built.
5. The bricks would keep the wood floor off the ground so it wouldn't get wet and warp.
6. The tarpaper was used to cover the roof so it wouldn't leak.
7. Yes, especially if there were small children around who might fall and get hurt.
8. You must answer this question yourself!
9. You must answer this one yourself too!

Questions to find out what you know about bullying:

1. Do you think it is funny to make fun of someone?
2. If your friend made fun of someone else, would you tell him or her to stop?
3. What if your friend got mad at you for telling him or her to stop?
4. Do you think everyone should be treated kindly?
5. Would you know how to help a student who was being mistreated?
6. What would you do to help a student who was being bullied?
7. If someone made fun of another student's clothes, would that be nice?
8. Would it be nice to make fun of the color of another person's skin or hair?
9. Should someone with a different accent be made fun of?
10. If someone is fat, should jokes be made about that person?
11. If someone is skinny, should people make comments about that person?

12. What if someone can't read very well? Should other students laugh?
13. Do you think everyone has a right to feel safe in school?
14. If you see a fight, should you tell your teacher (or bus driver or whomever is in charge)?
15. What if you see someone being mean on the bus to a student—is this bullying?
16. Should students call each other names? What about nicknames?
17. What if the student being called a name says to stop?
18. What if the name-caller doesn't stop?
19. If you see a student being taunted and that student doesn't report it, should you?
20. If you see someone has left his or her pencil holder on a desk, should you take it?
21. What would you do with the pencil holder?
22. If you see someone else take the pencil holder, should you report it?
23. What if the person who took the pencil holder gets mad at you? Should you report that person?
24. When you see someone who looks scared, what do you do?

25. Would you ask a frightened person if you can help him or her?
26. What if your friends laugh and make fun of you for helping a younger student? What would you do in that case?
27. What if a group of students pull things out of another student's hands and make the student chase them to get it back?
28. Is this group of students who took something out of another student's hands bullying or just having fun? How can you tell?
29. What if on the playground someone pushes you off the swing because he or she wants it? Is this bullying or playing around?
30. What is the difference between tattling and reporting bullying?
31. Should you respect someone who does mean things to others?
32. If someone is trying to talk, is it mean or rude to keep interrupting that person?
33. Is there any time when one student should hit another student?
34. Is there any reason why a student should be teased about his or her religion?

If you do not know the answers to **all** of these questions, then it is important to share the questions with your teacher and ask him/her what the rules of conduct are at your school. Maybe your interest will help your school toward establishing an Anti-bullying Code of Conduct!

INTRODUCING STUDENTS TO ANTI-BULLYING CODE OF CONDUCT

(To be Announced by Principal Watt
and Posted in All Classrooms)

We want Federal Street Elementary School to be a safe place. We don't want to worry about anyone being bullied or feeling afraid to be here. So, beginning right now, bullying is not allowed at school, on school property, on the bus, at the bus stop, or anyplace in between.

Bullying is doing anything that makes another person feel bad or feel scared about going to school or riding the bus. Also, if you see anyone acting like a bully, please report it to a member of Principal Watt's new Student Anti-bullying Committee so it can be stopped right away.

Remember, it is against the **Anti-bullying Code of Conduct** to keep bullying a secret. By not speaking up about bullying, the school doesn't know about it and can't stop it. So please, everyone sign the pledge to end bullying today!

FEDERAL STREET SCHOOL

ANTI-BULLYING CODE OF CONDUCT

I promise to respect other people and their property. I also promise to be respectful to my teacher and other people in authority.

I promise not to hit, trip, threaten, spit, fight, tell lies, gossip, taunt, razz, call names, or otherwise harass the students in this school. I promise not to fight, assault, or cause physical harm to students, teachers, and administrators. If I have a problem, or if I see someone being bullied, I will report it to a member of the Student anti-Bullying Committee.*

If I fail to act in accordance with this Anti-bullying Code of Conduct, I understand that there will be serious consequences for my actions.

Signed: _____   Date: _____

AUTHOR'S MESSAGE TO PARENTS AND EDUCATORS

Gone are the days when kindergarten was a place to learn social skills – where little Joey was required to share the crayons and not call people names, and timid Shirley learned to form a single line and take turns. Instead, five-year-olds are expected to begin "learning" immediately, and today's time constraints limit the emphasis teachers can put on social skills. Without these basic tools, many children do not know how to deal with normal childhood aggression and may respond inappropriately, or they may become victims – but they must learn when to "tell."

U.S. Department of Education's Office for Civil Rights (USDOECR) and the U.S. Department of Justice's Civil Rights Division (USJCRD) define bullying as unwanted, aggressive behavior among school aged children that involves a real or perceived power imbalance. The behavior is repeated, or has the potential to be repeated, over time. No matter what label is used (e.g., bullying, hazing, teasing) it includes making threats, spreading rumors, attacking someone physically or verbally, and excluding someone from a group on purpose.

While there is no Federal law that addresses bullying directly, bullying can overlap with discriminatory harassment in some cases when it is based on race, national origin, color, sex, age, disability, or religion. In this case Federally-funded schools have an obligation to resolve the harassment. When the situation is not adequately resolved, the USDOECR and the USJCRD may be able to help. (See: www.stopbullying.gov)

Schools must take prompt and effective steps reasonably calculated to end the harassment, eliminate any hostile environment, and prevent its recurrence. These duties are the responsibility of the school, even if this conduct is covered by an anti-bullying policy. Where no anti-bullying policy is in effect, a "Code of Conduct" would go far toward establishing a climate of learning all students need and deserve.

MaryAnn Milton Butterfield

*MEMBERS OF THE STUDENT ANTI-BULLYING
COMMITTEE:

Chuck

Michael

Jason

Joel

Andy

Matt

Nicole

Caroline

CPSIA information can be obtained at www.ICGtesting.com
Printed in the USA
BVOW07s0626100813

328096BV00001B/2/P